Mr. Monkey

Takes a Hike

Jeff Mack

Simon & Schuster Books for Young Readers

NEW YORK   LONDON   TORONTO   SYDNEY   NEW DELHI

For my dad, who loves a good hike!
Ooh! Ooh! Ooh!

SIMON & SCHUSTER BOOKS FOR YOUNG READERS
An imprint of Simon & Schuster Children's Publishing Division
1230 Avenue of the Americas, New York, New York 10020
Copyright © 2019 by Jeff Mack
SIMON & SCHUSTER BOOKS FOR YOUNG READERS is a trademark of Simon & Schuster, Inc.
For information about special discounts for bulk purchases, please contact Simon & Schuster Special Sales at
1-866-506-1949 or business@simonandschuster.com.
The Simon & Schuster Speakers Bureau can bring authors to your live event.
For more information or to book an event, contact the Simon & Schuster Speakers Bureau
at 1-866-248-3049 or visit our website at www.simonspeakers.com.
Book design by Chloë Foglia and Jeff Mack
The text for this book was set in Century Schoolbook.
The illustrations for this book were rendered digitally.
Manufactured in China
0119 SCP
First Edition
2 4 6 8 10 9 7 5 3 1
Library of Congress Cataloging-in-Publication Data
Names: Mack, Jeff, author, illustrator.
Title: Mr. Monkey takes a hike / Jeff Mack.
Description: First edition. | New York : Simon & Schuster Books for Young Readers, [2019] |
Series: Mr. Monkey ; [3] | Summary: Mr. Monkey takes a break from his favorite
video game to do something outside, but nothing goes as planned.
Identifiers: LCCN 2018012057 | ISBN 9781534404335 (paper over board) |
ISBN 9781534404342 (eBook)
Subjects: | CYAC: Monkeys—Fiction. | Video games—Fiction. | Humorous stories.
Classification: LCC PZ7.H83727 Mrq 2019 | DDC [E]—dc23
LC record available at https://lccn.loc.gov/2018012057

Mr. Monkey plays a video game.

He jumps.

He falls.

OOPS.

He loses.

GRR!

He tries again.

He runs. He ducks. He climbs.
He swings. He jumps. He falls.

He loses.

Poor Mr. Monkey.
He just can't win.

But wait.
What's this?

Mr. Monkey runs.

He jumps.

He falls.

OOPS!

He loses the bird.

Poor Mr. Monkey.
He just can't win.

But wait.
What's this?

He sees trees.

He sees flowers.

And he sees the bird!

But how will he get it?

He runs.

He ducks.

He climbs.

He swings.

He jumps.

He falls.

He gets it!

Look out,
Mr. Monkey!

Poor Mr. Monkey.
He just can't win.

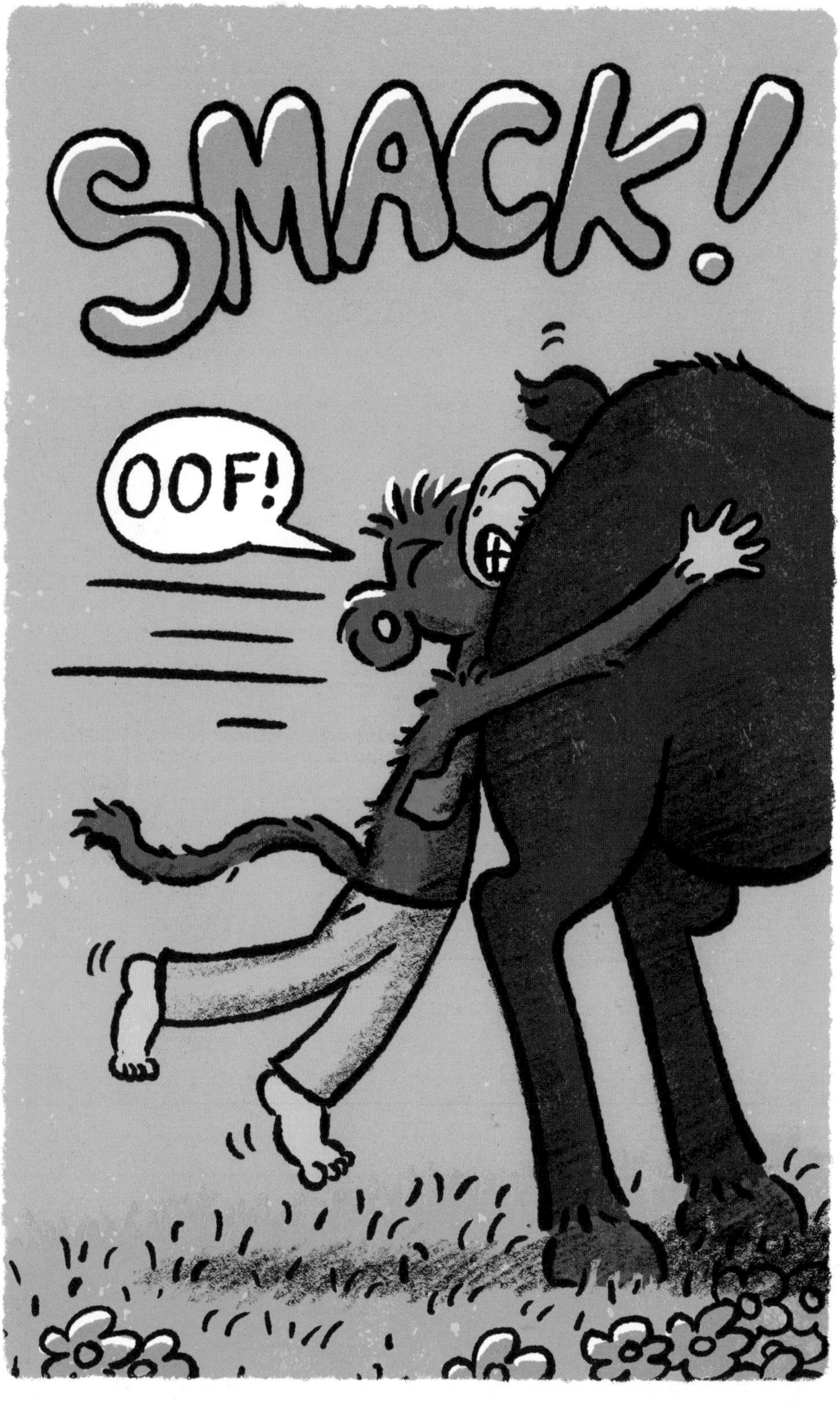
SMACK!
OOF!

Look out, Mr. Monkey!

Mr. Monkey runs.

He ducks.

He climbs.

He swings.

He jumps.

OOPS!

Poor Mr. Monkey.
Will he ever win?

No.
He just can't win.

Mr. Monkey sees mountains.

He sees clouds.

And he sees the bird.

He runs.

He ducks.

He swings.

He jumps.

And he falls.

The moose and
Mr. Monkey run.

They duck.

They climb.

They swing.

They jump.

all the way home.

It wasn't easy . . .

but Mr. Monkey did it.

He ran.

He ducked.

He climbed.

He swung.

He jumped.

He fell.

to win!

Good night, Mr. Monkey.